Marley O'Connor

Worlds Between Us

Dedication

This book wouldn't be possible without the support of friends and family.

To my mom for the endless encouragement. To my dad who always believed in his Goth.

To my children who show me to keep chasing my dreams.

To my boyfriend who always keeps me on track with his logical brain.

I love you all.

Table of Contents

Cover Page: 1
Copyright: 2
Dedication: 3
Table of Contents: 4
Prologue: 5
Chapter One: 7
Chapter Two: 17
Chapter Three: 28
Chapter Four: 36
Chapter Five: 45
Chapter Six: 47
Chapter Seven: 51
Chapter Eight: 55
Chapter Nine: 57
Chapter Ten: 58
Chapter Eleven: 62
Chapter Twelve: 67
Chapter Thirteen: 71
Chapter Fourteen: 73
Chapter Fifteen: 76
Chapter Sixteen: 78
Chapter Seventeen: 83
Chapter Eighteen: 87
Chapter Nineteen: 92
Chapter Twenty: 99
Chapter Twenty-One: 104
Chapter Twenty-Two: 107
Chapter Twenty-Three: 110
50 Years Later: 112
Afterword: 116

Prologue

Knocton

The spaceship was quiet as I and Uncle Nola observed planet Earth. It once was a vivid planet. Now it floated with a slight dullness.

"Knocton, this planet may seem like it is dying, but it always recovers. Even though it won't be as bright anymore. We have waited for this day. We found a planet that could sustain a new species. Our ancestors, the Sassani, came here long before us but only made a few humans pregnant. This time we will make our bloodline throughout this planet."

I watched as the excitement exploded in my uncle's eyes. He was never much of an emotional being, but I saw something rare right now.

"Yes, Uncle. But how?"

"Nephew, we will send you down in a ship that will eventually turn into space rock, causing a meteoroid to form. You will be fine. Our species are not human." Uncle Nola smiled.

"But if we come from The Sassani, we are part human. That means I can die."

"We do, but we can't be killed in such a quick manner. We bleed, yes. Our flesh is soft, yes. But it takes a lot to end our lives. We can go through a lot before we expire. So Knocton, you will go down to Earth. You will observe through the right vessel how that world is. You must make sure this vessel is the perfect fit. Once that is done, you come back here. I will take the vessel and make her the reproductive tool to make sure the remaining humans will slowly be enslaved while our Sassani bloodline rules the earth." He explains.

He held onto my shoulders with a grin. My heart grew heavy. Enslavement was never talked about during my parent's reign. He let go and snapped his fingers. Two of my fellow Sassani brothers came running through big metal doors into the large cockpit.

"Prepare the ship." Uncle Clapped.

Chapter One

Molly

The sky was dark that day. It has always been cloudy in Kansas City, but today it was dark, not gray. The wind softly blew the corn surrounding the crash scene.

"Molly, what is this? We've never covered something so X-files before."

I stood staring at a smoldering rock. The rock was a meteoroid that had fallen into the outer part of Kansas City. I stared heavily into the rock, my emerald eyes sparkling with wonder. The smoke invading my nostrils wasn't normal smelling. It smelled burned but with hints of vanilla.

"Ollie, what do you think? I'm surprised Ben wanted us to cover such a thing. I figured he wouldn't want some alien groupies coming for Lilac City Press."

"Yeah, that is strange. Maybe this little newspaper of ours is in trouble." He smirked, aiming his camera at an odd angle.

I gripped the end of my curly strawberry blonde hair twirling it around my index finger, taking in the scene. I glanced around and saw a detective observing the rock on the other side.

He had a charcoal-black military-style haircut, a stocky build, and piercing gray eyes. I grinned to myself. I could get this man eating from my hand. I had always been like a spell over men. With my curvy body and my Irish looks, men fell to their knees.

I left Ollie to his photograph and walked confidently over to the detective.

"Hello, I'm Molly Summers. I am a journalist for the

Kansas City Press or KPC to some. I would like to ask a few questions." I said under my lashes, holding my hand out.

The detective stared at me, unimpressed. Maybe my spell wouldn't work on this one.

"Sorry, Miss. Summers, but I don't do press."

He started to walk away but I wasn't one to back down, and I always got my story. I softly grabbed his arm.

"Wait, Detective-?"

" Parker. Parker Garrison." He sighed.

"Mr. Garrison, please. I don't need too much. Just when, where, and how?"

Parker hesitated for a moment. His eyes analyzed me. His distrust for the press swimming off him.

"Sorry, but the press never gets anything right. You all twist words and never put the truth in those articles. So no, I don't have your when, where, and how answers."

"Well lucky for you, I am a different kind of press. I seek the truth and bluntly publish it. Why do you think I am here? I'm the only one not scared of the consequences." Parker eyed me. I gave him my best beaming smile.

"Fine.

"This meteoroid fell from the sky in the early hours of the morning. A farmer who owns this land came checking on his stock when he saw this. That is all we have for now. Soon the fancy lab coats will have this case. Not many police businesses are needed. Now if you'll excuse me, I need to get back to the station."

"One more question before you go. I need the farmer's information. And no, I won't go annoying him. Pretty please." I pouted.

"Fine."

Parker wrote the farmer's information and slowly walked away. I watched as he left and giggled to myself.

"No one is safe from the Molly Summers spell, are they?" Ollie appeared from behind me.

I grinned at him and rustled his hair. He had boyish charm, loose curly blonde hair, and bright blue eyes. He was always dressed like he belonged to a prep school as a professor. His camera hung from his neck strap, and you would swear the thing was like another limb to him.

"No one at all Ollie. But some don't always fall for sensual charm, just my winning personality in general. Have you got all the pictures you need?"

"He was very handsome," Ollie trailed off but shook his mind into focus.

"But this is work, and I can't drool over man meat. But yes, I've got all I need. Are you ready to leave? I'm sure you blinked those green eyes and got all you needed."

"Of course, I got my leads. But I still haven't fully looked at the rock for myself. You know how I do things. My routine works. If it didn't, I wouldn't be the paper's best reporter."

Ollie rolled his eyes at my ego but followed me anyway. I studied the rock up close, taking in the deep shades of purple ember slowly dying.

"You know, I'm sure he's single Ollie. Maybe go ask him. How long has it been since you've been laid?" I giggled.

Ollie narrowed his eyes to me.

"First off, it hasn't been too long. Ben and I have been separated for only a few months. So maybe I've gotten some benefits from someone else. I have Grinder for a reason. Second, the way he was taking you in, I'm sure he's not interested in what I biologically have."

"Hmmm, I don't think he was taking me in the way you think he was. Yes, he was staring at me intensely, but I got the vibe he didn't know to trust me, but even if I'm wrong, men can be useless. I work to much anyhow."

"They can be sometimes useless, but they are fun for a good time if you know what I mean." Ollie winked.

I shook my head and continued studying the rock. Suddenly my eyes caught a small movement inside. I got closer. I could only see a little to the center.

There was a dense form of smoke inside. I gasped, staring into ember eyes. I heard Ollie press down on the camera behind me. As soon as he hit the capture button, the smoke came flying out and smashed through my nose.

I fell back. My head hit the ground. The pain cut through every nerve ending in my body and bone. I curled into a ball. My body felt like all my cells were going to explode at any minute. My bones screamed out as if someone was taking a hammer to each individual one but all at the same time.

"Molly? What the hell? SOMEONE HELP!" Ollie's frantic voice rang in my ears.

Ollie pulled me into his lap, rubbing my hair, still screaming for help. But every touch felt like fire. I began screaming from the pain. Footsteps raced towards me, and I realized Parker was still at the scene and heard Ollie's yelling.

He ran over and checked my pause. My vision started blurring, but worry struck his face as he pulled his phone out.

My vision became almost dark, and my hearing sounded like a tunnel. Ollie was sobbing, and Parker was speaking to 911.

"There is a woman on the south side of the outer part of the city. I need an ambulance asap. Her breathing is weak, and her pulse is weak. She collapsed in pain."

He hung up the phone and looked at Ollie and me.

"What's your name?" Parker asked sternly. "Oliver, Oli-Oliver Jones Sir."

Parker plastered a warm smile and placed his hand on Oliver's shoulder.

"Okay, Oliver. We need to keep watch on her breathing. Are there any health issues you're aware of that could have caused this?"

Oliver stared down at me. And started shaking his head. I wanted to comfort him, but I could no longer move. My body was on fire. My hearing and vision are almost gone.

"Okay. Well help is on the way. I'll stay with you."

Oliver nodded and held me tighter against his chest. The sirens were in the distance, breaking the air.

"They are almost here. See Oliver, it'll be okay." The ambulance pulled in and the medics jumped out. They raced over, pulling me from Oliver's arms. They placed a stethoscope on my chest. I screamed out in pain as it touched me and then the seizures started coming. I heard Oliver start crying harder.

"Turn her to the side. Wait it out."

I shook violently for a few moments and fell still.

"Check her breathing. She needs to be stable enough to transport."

I felt them press on my neck, and then they loaded me up; my vision was now in darkness.

My hearing was seconds from going.

Oliver's cries of protest traveled to me.

"Sir, you can't come with her. Only family is allowed."

"I am family. She has no one else."

"I'm sorry sir. But you can't. You can drive to the hospital."

The doors to the ambulance shut loudly. The powerful heat of my skin now felt like ice. I closed my eyes and started to let myself drift away.

But before consciousness left me, a beautiful voice spoke inside my head.

"It'll be okay, morning star."

Chapter Two

Molly

I'm lying in the hospital bed. The nurses were in and out, checking my vitals. My normally bouncy ginger hair lay frizzed around my shoulders.

The sounds of Oliver's voice float me awake. I looked over and gave him a small smirk.

"Hello, Ollie. What happened?"

I couldn't remember clearly what happened after Oliver's camera went off. All I remember is the pain and a voice, a mystery that was yet to be unraveled. Oliver laid his hand over mine, a comforting presence during confusion.

"The doctors said it seems like you just had a freak reaction. There is no damage to your body. But they don't want you to go back to work for a few days."

Oliver's eyes were wet. He had been crying. His baby blues were brighter when he cried, a testament to his deep concern for me.

"To hell with that Ollie. You know I can't work."

Oliver looked sternly at me, almost like an older brother would.

"You will do what the doctors say. You can write and research from home in bed."

I roll my eyes at him.

"Yeah, that's gonna be a no. How am I supposed to research anything? Do you really think some other newspaper hasn't picked up the story yet? We must be on this."

"Of course, they have. But that's how news works Molly. You can do everything from home."

"No. I will not." I protest.

I start to try and get up, but Ollie stops me. His eyes were wet again.

"You listen here Molly Eliza Summers. You could have died out there. I could have lost my best friend, my wingwoman, and my sister. I am your only family, so I will make sure you take care of yourself. I may not be any blood to you, but I am here. And you won't be doing anything risky. Do you understand?"

I stare at Oliver. I watch as tears fall on his cheeks. We've known one another since the foster care system. We managed to keep in contact after we turned eighteen. We even went to the same college and graduated, found the same job place. Ollie is my brother even if we share no blood.

There was a knock on the door, and we both looked up to find Parker standing awkwardly in the doorway.

"Ummm….is this a bad time?" He looked between us. "Oh. Shit. Sorry I forgotten. No, it's fine. Come in." Oliver said flustered.

Parker nodded and walked to the end of the bed.

"I needed your statement, Oliver. You rushed away before I could get it."

"Oh yes, sorry." Oliver blushed.

Parker smiled slightly. I watch them for a second, seeing a small spark light. A grin spread across my face. Oliver looked over and shook his head. He already knows what I'm thinking.

"So ummm…your statement?" Parker reminded.

Oliver sat back down, as Parker pulled out a pen and small notepad.

"Molly was up close to the rock, while we spoke. Sometimes I like to take pictures of her doing her job so I can add them to work themed galleries I do. But as soon as I clicked the camera, my flash went off. That's when she fell over. The doctors said there was no damage to her, and they aren't certain what had caused it." Parker nodded, writing every word down. After a few moments he shut his notepad and looked over at me.

"And how are you doing Miss. Summers?"

"Oh, peachy keen Officer Garrison. It seems you're doing just fine as well." I smirked.

"Well, that's all from me. Get well Miss. Summers." He started walking out but stopped in the doorway. "I'll be in touch." Parker said glancing quickly at Oliver before leaving.

I chuckle and Oliver glares at me. "What?"

"Seems like someone likes you, Oliver Leon Jones." "Oh whatever. Oh, look the doctor is here."

A doctor came into the room with discharge papers and went over my recovery instructions. I've always hated the recovery process of anything. It stops progress.

As the doctor left, Oliver started unpacking a small bag. He handed me a neatly folded pair of sweats and a sweatshirt. I grabbed them with disgust and stared at him.

"Yes, I did bring you sweatpants. Deal with it. Go change so we can get you home."

I roll my eyes but do as I'm told. A few minutes later I'm dressed like I haven't been out of the house in a month. I put my hands on my hips and glare at Ollie.

"God, why did you make look like an overworked college student again." I whined.

Oliver laughed.

"Oh, I'm just bringing out the person the makeup and fancy clothes hide. Finally, we can get out of here. Let's go. The car is up front."

I stuck my tongue at him and decided to give him the bird. We make it to the exit. Ollie's lilac sixty-five Mustang is waiting on us.

"Homeward bound Miss. Summers." Ollie smiles with relief.

The drive was smooth, and Oliver didn't talk which gave time for me to think about my article. We arrived at my apartment. My home was my favorite place.

It was always warm. The walls were all its original brick. The floors were all hardwood. And I had two big bay windows in the front. Only the third-floor apartments had those. It was perfect. Oliver led me to my room, helping me into bed. My room had the same walls and floors as the front room and kitchen.

But in here, it was my safety net. I slept in a queen-sized bed with bright yellow sheets and an orange comforter. My walls hung posters of famous authors and I had an old writing desk and a large oak bookcase.

Every day this place wraps me in its arms after a long day of pretending to be a hot-shot journalist. He made me soup and gave me my medication.

"Now I'm going to go text Barnett, so he reads it before morning, and I'll be back at lunch tomorrow. For now, only rest and tv. No moving all around or working. Got it?"

"Yesss Mom." I rolled my eyes and turned on the tv, sipping soup.

"Someone's got to look out for you Molly."

"Yeah, yeah, yeah. Go home. Oh, and make sure you pick up if Mr. Garrison calls." I wink.

Oliver shushes me away and closes my bedroom door before leaving. I stretched my arms out and snuggled underneath my heavy orange comforter. I flipped on Barbara Walters, and gently fell asleep.

---  ---

I wake to hear screaming. But my body feels heavy. I am no longer in bed.

I'm barefoot in my pjs surrounded by what looks like a desert. There are loud crashes and screaming all around me.

The sand is flying in the wind. I start pushing against the wind searching for people or anything to give me a clue to where I'm at. I walk for about five minutes when I see outlines of bodies in deep conversation. A small figure with three others hovering over. I step closer, trying to hear.

"Momma, why do you have to go? You don't need to stay and fight. Neither do you father. Let's go with Uncle. We can live." One of the shadows shakes their head. "Oh, my son, my sweet Knocton. I wish we could. But we are the leaders of this planet, so we must stay and fight with our army. We can't back down. Go with Uncle Nola, and the other children and their parents. Please, sweet boy. These monsters can't be contained much longer. They need us. And you must live. If we die, you must become the ruler over what's left of us."

I'm confused and move closer. I could now see them. They were beautiful, blue-skinned people. They looked human but they weren't. The male behind the boy had rough burgundy skin and black eyes, and no hair. The other older male was navy blue with sea green eyes and black hair, while the female was teal colored with golden amber eyes with long golden locks flowing down her back. The boy favored his mother.

"I do not want to be king. I don't want that title."

"I know Son. But as your mother said, it will be yours. I was king at the age of 8. Much younger than you are now. Be grateful to have such strong parents and an uncle. Be grateful you were a child longer than I. Now, Layla, we must go."

Layla looked deeply into her son's eyes. Tears welled into them, making them shine. She grabbed her son tightly against her and said her farewell.

"Till the endless stars, we shall never burn out." She stepped away.

The father nodded at Knocton.

"Are you ready Zidfree?" Layla asked. "Always ready for battle, my love."

They took one last glance at Knocton and ran off. Knocton screamed and tried to run after them but his uncle Nola grabbed him. He held him as he cried.

"We must go. We must keep you and what little people we have alive. You are not the only one to lose loved ones. I too will lose a sister. Come now Nephew."

I watch as the Nola man walks Knocton towards a ship. My vision slowly started fading, and soon darkness arrived.

---  ---

I woke up with a start. I tried to slow my breathing and touched my face. My cheeks were wet. I had been crying.

"What a weird dream." I say out loud.

I sat for a few minutes to collect myself. It was 2 am when I pulled my phone out. I still felt restless. So, I restarted my show on YouTube and tried to fall back to sleep.

Chapter Three

Molly

My sleep was restless since the first dream. The odd dreams were very faded, and the scenes confused me. They kept me turning. The sun slipped through the cracks of my blinds, waking me.

I glared at the sunlight but forced myself to sit up. My cheeks were wet once again, and my eyes were heavy. I shook my head trying to erase the dreams that now plagued my memory.

I dragged myself out of bed and into the bathroom. My bathroom is the only thing in this home that is in a modern style, and it's too white.

I never cared for plain things. I turned on my shower head, letting the water warm as I did my normal routine. I rinsed my mouth stripped my sweaty clothes to the floor and stood under the hot water, giving into the release of my tense muscles. I started humming a soft melody when suddenly someone whispered in my ears. My eyes shot open.

"Moollly…"

I threw open the curtain, but the bathroom was empty. I grabbed a towel, turned off the shower, and quickly walked into the living room. But that too was empty. I gripped my damp hair in confusion.

As I tried to make sense of it all, there was a knock at the door. I shook my thoughts away and raced to the door. Slowly I opened it, still uncertain of earlier experiences. Standing in his usual geeky clothes was Oliver. A bright grin and sparkling blue eyes welcomed me.

"HI! I have come with your favorite food, and some homework from Mr. B."

He walked around me, making himself at home. I smiled kindly as I watched him.

"Are you just gonna stand there? Or are you gonna go put some clothes on so we can go over this. Plus, Chinese is getting cold."

I rolled my eyes and ran to my room. I wasn't going anywhere so I chose my favorite PINK flower oversize sweatshirt, and my favorite pair of pink sweatpants. I combed through my long thick strawberry blonde hair with my slender fingers.

"Molly...."

The same voice from earlier whispered. I jumped from the mirror, searching the room. No one was there. Oliver was too busy setting work papers up for it to be him. I ran my hands down my face in worry.

"Get it together, Summers." I whispered to myself.

I pulled on some socks over my white painted toe-nailed feet and went out to Oliver.

"What took you so long?" Oliver frowned.

"Sorry, I was just checking out my unprofessional clothes." I smiled.

"Well, sorry but sweats till Monday, and no wine either." I groaned at him in annoyance. He was always treating me like some glass doll.

"Fine. But next weekend we are getting trashed." I spoke. wickedly.

Oliver rolled his eyes and handed me some papers. I took them and studied one at a time. One was witnesses Oliver somehow retrieved. The other was pictures of the crash site. The site was empty of media personnel and cops.

The only people in the photos were men in lab coats. They had devices scanning the rock and the field surrounding it. The pictures were taken from the above vantage point.

"How did you get these?"

Oliver proudly grinned and pulled out a small drone.

"With the Christmas gift you got me last year."

I smiled.

I had forgotten about that gift. Oliver gasped and rummaged through his laptop bag.

"I forgot I had one more picture. It was taken by a witness on the list. She was up when the rock came into view. She just so happened to be on that road, looking at stars."

He pulled out another picture and handed it to me. The picture was dark, but the focus lit up orange like fire. *"From home…"* That same voice rang out.

I jumped a little and dropped the picture. Oliver touched my shoulder with concern.

"Molly, are you okay? What's wrong?"

"You didn't hear that?"

"Hear what? Molly, what's wrong?"

"I… Oh, never mind we have work to do."

Oliver frowned at me. I knew I could hardly ever get away with a lie around him.

"Molly, you can't lie to me. What is wrong?"

"Nothing. I had some nightmares. I'm still shaken by them. Really, I am fine. So, were all these people contacted?"

Oliver sighed, knowing I wouldn't talk about the issue again, and started explaining.

"Yes. But because you have an uncanny way of bringing out secrets, I told them you'd like to take their statements yourself. I told them I would ask you since you are sick how you'd like them to contact me. Phone or maybe a home visit

interview. If its home, Mr. B said I could be present."

I thought this over. Of course, the home interview is the best. I work my magic with eye connection.

"We can set up the home interview. Tell Barnett thanks." "You know he will do anything for his best journalist." "Sure. Well good job to you as well. How did you do all this?" Oliver blushed and ran his hands through his hair.

"All I can say was you were right. And I didn't do it all on my own. But I gotta head back. So, rest up, heat up your food, and then work. Be careful, and call if you need me." "Of course, moooom" I joked.

Oliver stuck his tongue out at me and left. I sat on the couch looking over everything. I went back to the falling rock. I rubbed my finger across the picture.

A longing I didn't understand slowly crept over me. I ran my hands through my hair, and then tied it up. I made my way to the kitchen with the food. Once it was heated, I grabbed all the papers, and my MacBook. I didn't want to use my desk tonight, so I decided to work on my bed.

I took my pills, grabbed my tv remote, and placed a rerun of the office in the background, and went to work in between food. After eating and trying my best to work through the pain killers, I finally fell into the darkness.

Chapter Four

Molly

Monday came like thunder. I wanted to stay in bed, but I had already slept most of the weekend. Now it was time to get back to work.

I pulled on my forest green pantsuit. I decided on my favorite pair of ebony Jimmy Choo's and headed for the bathroom. I stared at myself. Dark circles hugged under my eyes. I sighed.

This incident had hit my face hard. I decided a full face with neutral colors and no bright lipstick would do. I tightened my long hair in a high ponytail and went off to work.

---  ---

As I walked through the doors, it felt like home. The building was spacious with brick walls and two large casement windows beside the front door.

It was placed in between an insurance corporation and art studio. The desks were spread out like you'd see in old black and white detective movies. I smiled as reached my desk. There was a pile of get-well cards on top of the cherry oak desk. I grabbed them up and started reading them.

"Hi ya, kiddo. How are you?" A husky southern voice said.

John Barnett smiled. He was in his mid-fifties. He wasn't from Lilac but from Kentucky, Ohio. His accent was still strong. His hair was gone on top, but still clung white on the sides and mid back of his head.

His eyes were always warm chocolate. He treated me like his daughter. I jumped from my chair and hugged him. It always felt like hugging a big stuffed teddy bear.

"I'll take that as a yes. So, what are we doing today?"

I pulled back and took out the papers from Oliver.

"I want to input all the interviews Oliver and I did Sunday. But I want to check out the crash scene first."

"Oliver is off today. But I can call him in."

"That's okay. I can do this myself John. I feel much better."

John rolled his eyes but agreed.

"Well, it rained last night, so put on some jeans, and tennis shoes. Your Barbie clothes aren't gonna hold up to those muddy fields." He smiled.

I nodded. I opened my desk drawer, placed my cards inside, and grabbed my bag. The break room had a small locker room.

I stepped inside and pulled on my jeans and my thin long sleeve shirt from my locker. I ran back through the desk, waving bye to John and headed out.

---  ---

As I made my way to the scene, I noticed the skies were a bit brighter than they have been. The weather has gone late spring, replacing it with a wet warmth.

I parked my pink Volkswagen bug on the side of the dirt road and started walking to the site. The rock had been taken away, but the markings of it were still scorched into the ground.

I bent down rubbing the mark. It was ash. But within the ash, some flakes of dark purple reflected on my fingertips. That same soft hint of vanilla still hung in the air. I pulled my papers out and studied them.

Several people saw it falling, but that's it. And only one person had a picture of it mid falling. I stared at the papers, trying to figure out my next move.

"Molly….Come…. Come to me…."

I jerked my head back. That same voice floated in my ears. A warm presence felt like they had been right behind me, whispering into my ear.

I stood slowly, looking around, and in the distance, A good amount of distance into the field, I seen a blurry figure. My instincts told me to run, but I've never been one to say no to a challenge or mystery.

So, I ran towards it. The figure just stood there staring at me. I was almost there, only a couple feet away, when the figure disappeared.

I stopped straight in my tracks. I almost lost footing in the muddy field. I looked around, confused.

"What the hell?"

Suddenly my body felt warm. My stomach cramped, causing me to collapse. I felt like something was crawling under my skin. Then all sense of movement was gone. I tried to move but nothing happened.

All I could do was watch. I saw a memory that wasn't mine. I see two men but not like any human, almost alien. They were on a ship and speaking. The earth was in front of the window. I shook as I watched.

"Nephew, go to earth. We need more of our kind. Find a vessel. Make sure she is good. We will use her to create more, and we will enslave the rest. Earth will be our new home."

The memory was gone, and I was left shaken.

"What is going on? Am I losing it? Why can't I move my body? What's happening?"

Then out of the blue the same voice came back to me.

"Molly, I am Knocton. I am in control. I see our shared presence can show you, my memories. I wonder if the same is with you. As you saw, that is my mission. No harm will come to you. Now I am on the second step of my mission. When you wake, you will be home in your bed. Now go to sleep Molly."

"Wait-" I yelled.

But darkness only responded inside my eyes.

---  ---

I awoke in my bed, just as Knocton said. I grabbed myself making sure I was here. I felt like I was going crazy. I didn't understand what was happening and why it was happening. I sat on my bed rocking.

I hadn't felt this lack of control since childhood in foster homes. I never thought I'd feel that again until now.

As I sat wondering what happened, my phone buzzed. I looked down and saw six missed calls from John. I pressed his contact and called.

"What the hell Molly! Where have you been? Are you okay?"

"Yes. I'm not sure what happened. I was at the site, then I thought I passed out and I woke up at home. I saw someone in the field, and I ran after them. But they disappeared and I blacked out."

There was silence as John processed the information.

"Kiddo, I don't think you should have come in today. I'm giving you mandatory medical leave with pay for a month. Figure out whats going on. Something was triggered in that seizure. And no, I won't hear any back talk. This is an order not offer. Olli can handle this. Keep me update."

Before I could protest, John hung up. I sat on my bed, staring at the brick walls. Tears fell onto my cheeks. My mind felt foggy and heavy. I was losing energy, hearing voices. I;m having memories that weren't my own.

I pulled myself off my bed and went to my closet. I found my fluffiest pajamas and stared at myself in the mirror.

"Is this what I'm becoming? An insane PJ wearing soon-to-be ex journalist?"

More tears streamed down my face. I held my face in my hands, sobbing.

"Molly…." Knocton's cool voice rang out.

I slowly lifted my head, and in the mirror stood Knocton. His azure skin was luminous. Small flecks of what look like stars shined in his skin.

His eyes were shining amber orange, and his hair was shaggy and gold. His face was kind, and soft. My eyes couldn't understand the beauty of him.

"Why? Why me? Why do you want to use me to

populate your kind? This is inhumane. It's disgusting. For such a beautiful creature, what you want is so dark, and ugly."

Knocton floated from the mirror and kneeled in front of me. I gasped, taken back. I stared into his eyes. Wonder but sorrow clouded them.

"We are a dying breed."

And just like that he was gone, and a rush of air and goosebumps flowed through my body. I stayed shaking on my bed. The familiar fear from childhood rose through and paralyzed me.

I felt like a child again. Felt as if I was hiding in the foster family's closet. I was afraid all over again. I couldn't control anything, just like I couldn't control the anger and beatings I received at each home I was placed in.

I slowly regained myself and fell into my bed. I snuggled the thick warm orange comforter over me. I gently fell asleep.

Chapter Five

Knockton

I was standing beside a child Molly. She had rolled in on herself, hands over her hand. She pleaded with a round older woman. Venom spilled from her eyes.

"Please Mrs. Luster. I was hungry. I didn't mean to take it without asking." "I do not care, Molly. This is punishment. You will learn to obey and listen."

I watched as a small Molly was beaten for several minutes. Mrs. Luster left Molly on the bedroom floor bleeding and weeping.

"I wish I was dead. This wouldn't happen if I were dead. I have no family." Little Molly cried.

I bent down and stared at her. My eyes filled with sorrow, and my heart ached. I wanted to reach down, and assure it was okay. I wanted to protect her.

I wanted to make her feel like she was loved and would be safe. But this feeling was new to me. I hadn't felt that in a long time. I watched as child Molly unrolled herself and made her way to the closet.

She sat down in the back corner, revealing a small journal under a loose floorboard. I slowly made my way to her side again. I watched as she wrote down her heart's cries.

"One day, I will be far far away from this place. I will be away from families who don't want me. My skin won't be bruised, and my eyes won't dry from crying too much. One day I'll fly away, no longer captive."

I reached my hand to touch her cheek, but it just went through her. I was in her dream, that was a memory. I couldn't help her, comfort her. Even if I could touch her, or comfort her, could I?

My mission was beginning to feel like this memory. I was caging her again, taking her wings. Making her unable to fly away. A sudden pulse violated through me. My body felt heavy. The scene was fading, and I heard Molly's heart racing. She was waking up.
Suddenly I saw blackness, and Molly jumped awake from her dream

Chapter Six

Molly

"I hate that nightmare." I gasped.

I wiped my tears and sat looking at the closet mirror. Last night was still a huge confusion in my mind.

I couldn't fathom what I had seen, last night. Maybe the seizure had done more damage than I realized. I shook my thoughts away and got dressed. It had been a while since I had a run. So, I threw on some leggings and a tank. I pulled my hair in pigtails and took off out the door.

---  ---

The morning air was warm and inviting. The burn in my legs was most welcomed. I loved my city. It wasn't too small, but it wasn't extremely big.

I ran a trail that wasn't as trailed as most of them. It had the perfect view of the sun rising. I got to the cliff and stood watching. The sky turned sherbet orange and pink. Birds were chirping and for the first time, I felt good.

"This is beautiful Molly." I jolted a little and sighed.

"I am definitely losing it."

I ran back into the city. I grabbed a coffee from Starbucks and headed home. Once I was home, I took a shower and put another pair of fluffy pjs on and fixed lunch.

As my fish was cooking, I pulled out my laptop, and started researching aliens.

"That isn't all true. You humans are so creative."

I shook her head, ignoring Knocton's voice. I pulled my fish from the air fryer and took my research and food to my desk. I searched and searched.

Eventually, I fell asleep, alien videos playing on YouTube.

--- 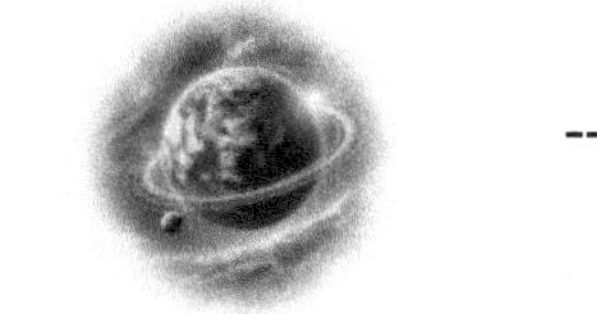 ---

"Molly, I am here. You must believe me. Look at me."

I found myself floating in space. My heart started racing. Fear flowed through me. Then Knocton appeared, taking my hands. I stared into his eyes. The amber gold soothed me.

"Wh-where am I?"

"This is a space where we can speak easier. I can touch you. Humans seem to like to have conversations with something they can touch." He smiled kindly.

I jerked my hands out of his and floated a little away from him. I looked anxiously around him.

"Why did you bring me here? Get out of my dreams, my mind. Stop invading me. If this is even real."

"Molly, I am real. I am from out here. From a different galaxy. My ancestors had human blood in them. They came here a long time. ago. They mated with a few humans to keep us going. That is our goal."

I shook my head. I remembered what that other man said.

"No. I heard it, and I saw your memory. You and your uncle want to keep getting me pregnant to take over this earth, then enslave the rest. That won't happen."

"We will not enslave them. We will rule over them. Like your president or any other person in power. You will be treated as a queen. Mother of our people, of our new generation."

"I refuse. I'll kill myself if I must. You won't use me. I won't use again. I am an adult now. I am stronger. I will never allow someone to hurt me against my will. **Certainly not an alien.**"

My fists were clenched so tightly, that my fingernails dug into my palms/ The space we were in was beautiful. If he was a shade of dark blue instead of baby blue, all I could see of him would be his eyes.

His eyes were just as bright as the stars in his skin and surrounding us. But they also looked at me with sadness. I could feel him waiting to speak so I floated, waiting.

Chapter Seven

Knockton

I looked at her with sadness. I remembered the dream from the other night. remembered the beating Molly took. That same feeling claimed my heart. I walked to her, holding her face in my hands. What was this feeling in my chest?

I've never experienced this before. I've had lovers. As a king, they expect you too. But this was never there. Thie ache to hold her and keep her safe.

The mission I know would put her in harm's way. My heart and body were at war. I wanted to hide her way, but my duty as king kept screaming in my ears.

A pounding from outside our sacred realm filled my senses. Oliver's heartbeat filled my senses. But Molly seemed to be too consumed with begging me to rethink my plan. I held her face and touched her forehead with mine.

"You do not understand right now but I promise you will, now. Molly, it's time to go. Oliver is here."

And with that, I vanished the space gone, and a banging rang through her ears. I feel Molly jerk away, shaking my words from her mind.

Oliver's yells pierced her ears.

"MOLLLY??? HELLO??? OPEN UP!" Oliver shouted.

Molly rubbed her eyes and ran to the door. She threw it open to see Oliver and Parker staring at her. Oliver was red with anger and worry. Parker looked embarrassed.

"Really Oli? You had to bring the police?" Molly rolled her eyes.

She stepped away to let them in.

"Mr. B called me. He told me what was happening, and the medical leave. Why didn't you call me?"

"I've been sleeping a lot, okay. Don't worry." Molly said flopping on the couch.

Oliver stood in front of her, hands on his hips.

"I don't care. I saw the running clothes Molly; I smelled the fish. You went running and made lunch. You could have called between all of that."

"I'm-" Oliver cut her off.

"No, you scared the hell out of me. I'm here. I care. Why didn't you call?"

Molly looked at her folded hands. I sense her emotions trying to build a wall.

"It was your day off. You already do so much for me. Worry too much. I didn't want to bug you."

Oliver's jaw dropped and he took her into a tight hug and spoke into her hair.

"Don't you ever think you are bugging me, or that I am doing too much for you. You are my sister, blood or not. I love you. I'm not in those families. I'm not the parents who gave you up." Molly nodded.

And like that, she started sobbing into Oliver. All the stress released into him. He held her tighter.

I felt her heartbreak pouring into my being. Guilt cascaded through me. I wanted to be the one to hold her. But my mission was to come first, even if that meant breaking my heart.

"I'm sorry Molly." my voice was a whisper in her mind.

Molly nodded at my voice and pulled away from Oliver. She wiped her eyes and softly smiled at Oliver. Then she turned her attention to Parker.

Chapter Eight

Molly

"So, he really called you for backup?"

He smiled and shook his head.

"Umm…actually we were on a date." Parker's face blushed.

I turned to Oliver, grinning like The Joker.

"So, I was right." I gloated.

Oliver rolled his eyes and shoved me lightly.

"That's not the issue here. Are you okay?"

I looked out the window, remembering the space with Knocton. How even though I know what he wants me for, I still seemed okay when he touched me.

He made it feel safe when his hand rested on my cheek. He made it feel as though he was there, maybe I would be okay giving my body up.

"I will be. Do you guys want to stay over? I've been told my couch is heaven sent. I'm ordering Pizza and watching Grease."

"Oh, you know those are two of my weaknesses Molls." Oliver grinned.

"Parker?" Oliver asked.

"Yeah. I haven't seen grease before. I'm more of an action flick kind of guy."

"Oh, then you must watch carefully. I'll go order." I smiled

Chapter Nine

Molly

Oliver and Parker had fallen asleep on the couch, and I on the chair. The was room silent. The movie had ended and was playing on the title screen. The silence woke me. I hated the quiet.

The quiet reminded me of the days I'd spend writing in my many closets, hiding from the beating or lectures. I looked over and smiled at the boys. I had a feeling this one would be good for Oliver.

I sleepily drag myself to my room, turning on the fan, and dropping under the covers. my eyes were still heavy. with sleep.

"Molly…Close your eyes and come to me."

His voice sounded sweet and calming. Slowly I let my eyes fall shut.

Chapter Ten

Knockton

I waited for her to come floating in. I tried my best to not disturb her when Oliver or anyone else was around. Before I even saw it, I knew she had appeared.

I felt the light flooding into my darkness, waking me. Her hair was in wild curls down her back, and her emerald, green eyes pierced into me. I slowly moved towards her. My height towering towards her. My species was much taller than humans.

"Why am I here Knockton?"

"I wanted to speak with you."

"About what? More about how I'm going to be your sex slave. My freedom along with my species, stripped away. That what you wanna speak on?"

My eyes dropped, and my thoughts turned. I never really thought much about my uncle's plan. I did not know how to run a kingdom. So, I let him lead me.

The more she speaks about his plan, the more this feeling in my chest grows for her. I want to reach out and protect her. I lift my head, and my eyes burn into hers. Guilt, and torment lay beneath mine. Sorrow and panic fill hers. A part of me hates this plan, but what else can I do? I would make this world better, safer.

I come closer to molly. She wants to walk back but she's frozen. I can feel all her emotions. I can see all her insecurities, and all her trauma. Her beauty is intoxicating. I gently cup one side of her face in my right hand, searching her face. Something vibrating inside my chest, creating a need to hold her.

"I don't want to hold you captive, Molly. I rather you come of your own accord. But humans, they are if anything stubborn. You bend at your own agenda. I have looked at this planet for centuries. From afar, I've witnessed wars, millions of deaths. I've heard the cries of mothers whose children are ripped from them. I've seen men sell young boys and girls into buyers. I have seen wickedness and all of its sickness. Humans use this planet like a wasteland. They treat their kin like the very dirt they step on. And you see, this is why this plan works. We will create a better life on this planet. No war, not a terrible end, no sex trafficking, no more worthless deaths."

Molly stared into my eyes; hope filled them. Hope that she can convince me otherwise.

"As nice as you make it sound, that's not what you'll be doing. Humans don't lie down and bow to anyone. You'll have to control us, take away our rights. Then we will become shells. We won't be human any longer. I saw your memory. War is what made you an orphan like me. So, I see where you are coming from, but that doesn't make this right."

Sorrow stung my eyes. Flashes of mother and father fall into my mind. I hold her, staring into the stars.

Molly moved closer to me. She touched my arm. Electrics shocks move to my heart. The feeling is foreign to me and intense.

"An enslaved life is not a life at all, Knock."

Tears streamed down her face. I slowly wipe them away.

"You won't be enslaved. You'll be honored. But our time here is over for now. You'll be with me soon."

With a snap of my fingers, I sent her awake.

Chapter Eleven

Molly

And with that, darkness clouds the space and I'm sent back. I wake the next morning to Oliver shaking me awake. I slowly opened my eyes to find panic in him. I jerk up staring at him.

"What's wrong? What's going on?"

There on the screen is our news reporter. In the sky behind him, looks as if there is a metal ship.

"As you see behind me, up in the sky is a UFO. Yes people, a real UFO. It was reported in the early hours of the am. It hasn't moved since, and we have word that special forces are coming."

Oliver sat on my bed; worry spread against his whole being. My thoughts drift to the last conversation with Knockton. I had hoped he would change it.

He said this would happen. But I had seen pain, guilt and doubt in the plan they spoke of. I stared back at Oliver, trying to find the words that I might know about that ship.

"What the hell is happening, Molls? It has to do with that rock we were making an article on."

I grabbed Oliver's hand and held it tight, trying to find the words to explain this. He's staring at me. Confusion spread about him.

 "Ollie, I may be part of this." He grabs my other hand. "Huh? What do you mean?"

I breath in.

"When I fell ill that day at the site, it was a freak accident. But it had nothing to do with my health. It was the rock."

Oliver thought this over, gripping my hand tighter.

"What? What are you saying, Molls?"

"I'm saying, there was a being in that rock. When I fell, it was him who came into my body. There is an alien inside me. He plans to use me to populate the earth and take dominance over humans."

Oliver stares at me in shock. He removes his hand from mine.

I stall myself for him to declare my insanity.

"Ollie?"

"Molls, I don't know what to say."

"Please say you believe me. After seeing that report, I know I'm not crazy. He's real, and he wants me."

Oliver stands from my bed and goes to stare out my window.

He is all tense, and his presence is frigid.

"I can show you. I can show you Knockton." I declare.

He turns around and stares at me. His eyes are unreadable. He moves to the door. I fist my hands, and whisper for Knocton to become solid and show himself.

But for the first time in a month, I don't feel his presence in me. I feel empty.

"Molly, I wish I could believe you. But you are just another human like me and the rest of the world. You fell ill, and you've been different since. I don't believe that ship is here for you."

He grabs my bedroom door handle and starts to walk out. I jump from my bed, grabbing his arm.

"Please Ollie. I'm not crazy. I'm telling the truth." Oliver pulls me into a hug, and sighs.

"You've been through a lot, Molly. Maybe the trauma you thought was healed, isn't. I don't know what's going on out there, but right now you need to figure out what's going on in your head. I'll call if John knows anything. But for now, stay home."

Oliver lets me go and walks out of my apartment. I stand in shock. Oliver has always believed me. My chest aches. I know I'm not crazy.

I've felt Knockton hold me, I've seen his memories and felt his sadness. Suddenly I'm pulled from my thoughts. A burning sensation spreads across my body, and my head starts to pound. Smoke is pouring from my skin.

I lay on my bed as I watched Knockton materialize in front of me. His beauty hits me, making me forget the pain. His somber eyes watch me.

"What? How are you here? I called for you. I needed you to show Ollie, but now he thinks I'm crazy."

"I had to ignore that. I had to make you think I left. But it's time for the last task of the mission, Molly." I shake my head.

"No, I won't do it. I'm not a slave. This is my body. And I'll be damned if I let someone else tell me what to do with it again."

I back against my bedroom door. My body becomes all fight. My hair flies wild around me as I try to fight Knocton off me. My face is soaked with tears, and my body trembles. Knocton finally has me in a hold. He holds my forehead to his like before.

"Molly, calm down. Please. Let me help you."

I try to protest but my body begins to feel like led and my eyes drop. I fell into a slumber in Knocton's arms.

Chapter Twelve

Knocton

I put Molly to sleep. The same way Uncle did to the first month of my parent's dying. I flew us up onto my ship. I laid Molly in my bed and placed the covers over her. I stared at her with sadness.

I know what she's pleading me with is true. My whole body wants to fight against it, but my people are dying, my kingdom needs a new home.

She is the key Uncle says. I must listen to his wisdom. I touch her face, and kiss her forehead, leaving her to meet with Uncle.

Uncle is standing at the windows, facing the city. His hands are behind his back, studying the ant sized humans.

"Weak things, aren't they?'

He turned smiling at me. His words turned my stomach. I had never seen this side of Uncle before. I had heard mother and father speak with him above his views.

But it was always in hushed whispers. My mother and father wanted to live in peace with all worlds and species. They only went to war when necessary. But Uncle had blood lust draining from his pores now.

"Actually, these humans are stronger than they look. Interesting creatures."

Uncle lifted an eyebrow at me, and let out a loud laugh, lightly smacking my back.

"Do you think? I'm not sure they are strong or interesting. I've seen some of the things they have made and enjoy. And some of those things have little intelligence."

I watched as Uncle took a seat on my throne. He rarely did that but today was different. He was different.

"But enough with the humans and their hobbies. What of the vessel you required? Is she here? Did you bring her here?"

I hesitated.

There was now a hunger in Uncle's eyes I had never seen before. My heart raced, and that need to protect Molly came spiraling into my gut.

"Yes. But she needs her rest. She's been through a lot." Uncle stared at me for a few minutes, and then slowly removed himself from my throne.

He walked to me, placing his hands on my shoulder like many times before. But this time, it was more of a grip, his nails tearing into my skin.

"Make sure she is up and alert. and dressed in an hour. No excuses."

Before I could reply, Uncle had already made his way to the door. He glanced back at me. His eyes sent a spark of terror into my gut. But not for me but for Molly. Something is off. This plan has more than I knew about. Regret and guilt pollute my heart.

I watch him make his way to his chamber and walk to my own. On my desk is a gold-colored knee length dress. I ran my hands over it. It's soft and it sparkles. I turned my attention to Molly. She's still asleep. This is the calmest sleep I've seen her have. No nightmares plague her.

I walked over, sitting on the edge of the bed. I touched her hand,waking her from the sleep I had cast.

Her eyes slowly opened and took in the scene. Her eyes grew big, and she jolted upwards. Fear coated her pores. I reached out to her, but she pushed me away.

"Where the hell am I, Knoc?" *"My ship. Its time."*

"No. Let me go. Please."

I stare into her glassy eyes. The emerald cutting into my very soul. I grab her hands, gently stroking her knuckles.

"I am sorry, Molly. But I am a King, and my kingdom, my people need me."

Tears began streaming down her face. The tears make her eyes even more green than they are naturally. I dropped her hands and grabbed the dress. I laid it in front of her. I cup her cheek, and kiss her forehead, my heart shattering.

Chapter Thirteen

Molly

I stare down at the shimmering dress. Tear drops fall on the material causing some of the glitter to sparkle. The material is soft, and sheer. Laying still on the desk are white boy short underwear and a cami.

I stare around me. Knocton's room is bare. The only thing that looks as if it has sentimental value is a small trinket on his desk. I stand up, placing the dress back on the desk. The trinket is a crystal.

The same color and shine of his skin. The crystal wasn't smooth. It was jagged at different edges and seemed to have been hacked off an edge roughly. I touch every side of it, taking in all the color and shine.

I stared at it for a few minutes and placed it where I grabbed it from. I turned my attention back to the dress. Breathing in deeply, I put on the underclothes and then slipped the dress on.

There is a full-length mirror on the other side of the room, so I slowly walk towards it. Reflected in the mirror is the beautiful gown. It hugs my curves perfectly. My hair matches well with the color, and the length is just right. Long enough to be intriguing but short enough that I don't fall.

Suddenly, my body tenses, and I can feel him coming into the room. We are no longer sharing my body, but I can still sense his presence, his soul.

He makes his way to me, standing behind me. His ember eyes take me in. Drinking in my reflection. I look into his eyes, and I catch sadness. His demeanor is full of it. I turn around and touch his chest. It's firm and muscular. I looked into his eyes.

"What is wrong, Knoc?"

He shakes his head and rests his forehead on mine.

"Nothing, morning star. Let's go. It's time."

He grabs my hand and tucks me beside him.

Chapter Fourteen

Knocton

She is stunning. My stomach is on fire, and my heart pulls. The dress hugs her perfectly. My instincts want to keep her tucked beside me, away from this plan. But I am a King, and a King must put duty over emotions.

I can feel her fear soaking from every fiber of her body, as we make our way to the command center. Our bodies are now separate, but we are still attached.

Our souls are now intertwined with one another. I look at her from the corner of my eye and see her staring off. Her heart is racing, and I know there is no way I can calm it. As I slowly walk us down the hall, trying to calm my own heart, she speaks.

"Will this help you?"

Her question stuns me for a moment. She was hell bent against her role, but now it seems as if she's willing.

"It will help my people, my kingdom. Have you changed your mind?"

She stops us and looks up at me.

"Who gave you the crystal on your desk?"

My mind brings the crystal to the center. The crystal my mother gave me on a forge lesson a year before the battle that killed her. An ache grabs my heart.

"My mother gave it to me. We were in the middle of a forge lesson, and she cut it off in one of our mines. It was a year before the battle that killed her, my father, some of our commoners, and our greatest warriors."

Her stare is soft and understanding. I wish I could have the same effect on her. But I've only caused her fear. She moves her hand to my cheek, rubbing her thumb over it.

"The memory of your last moments with her, you look a lot like her. You seem to take after her a lot more than your father."

"My father was a very loud, and silly man. He was an honest, true and kind King. But I was always quiet. An observer in the background, my nose in a book. I never wanted to be a ruler. I would have been very content studying the stars." I chuckled.

She grinned up at me. Her heart had calmed down, and the fear lessened. She removed her hand from my face. She twined her arm into mine and leaned her head on my bicep.

"I believe in fate, destiny. I know we can make it whatever we want. But some fates are not able to change. If this is my unchangeable fate, and it is with you, I'll accept it. I believe you will be a true and kind king. I believe you can help my people, as much as I will help yours."

My eyes grew wide, and my heart thumped even louder. This human, one I've grown to become attached to, understanding the role of a king, and believing in me racks me. I'll be constantly surprised by humans for the rest of my life.

"Well? Are you ready to save your people?"

Molly smiles at me I can't find the words to say, so I nod.

Chapter Fifteen

Knocton

I led her into the command center. I looked to her for her reaction. I thought this room would make her eyes wonder. But instead, she focused on my uncle, who once again sat on my throne.

I patted her arm lightly, and she broke her eyes from him to me.

"I must talk to Uncle."

I let go of her arm and walked slowly to my uncle. He never once stopped looking at Molly. There was a dark hunger in his eyes. My insides flared with fear for her.

My inner voice shouted at me that something was wrong. My whole body seemed to want to be on the defensive for her. I wanted to stand in front of her, blocking the hungry eyes that drilled into her body.

"Uncle, what is next? Molly has spoken on the news reports. We can send our own broadcast. Tell them we mean no harm."

"We shall do no such thing."

I stood in confusion. The plan was to take Molly. She was to be my bride. Make more of our kind, and then make the earth better. Make earth the way our kingdom once was.

To bring our kingdom here, so the earth and our people would prosper. Uncle removed himself from my throne and started walking towards Molly. Molly stared at me and back to Uncle. I could feel her fear returning but she showed no signs on her face.

Chapter Sixteen

Molly

I watched as Knocton's Uncle approached me. He didn't look like Knocton. His skin was the color of fire, and his eyes were cold. His whole being felt like death.

The way he bore his eyes into me now sent chills through my body. He walked around me, licking his lips. His eyes drank in every part of my body. I stared at Knocton, silently pleading for his help. But his eyes just filled with concern and regret.

"What a fine breeding vessel you have gathered, Knocton. She will do finely."

I stared at him. He looked nothing like Knocton. His skin was a deep burgundy rough, and small black mole were randomly placed. His eyes were the color of coal and held no warmth. His smile was venomous.

He reached out his hand and touched his fingertips to my arm. My body recoiled, and I moved away from him. I moved closer to Knocton.

His body instantly warmed mine. And I felt safe. Standing by his uncle felt like death had wrapped me in his cloak. Knocton held me to his side.

His arm wrapped around my waist. He looked down at me, with a soft smile. My heart raced when his eyes fell into mine.

"My dear Nephew, it seems this human likes you."

I felt Knocton's hold on my waist tightening, but not enough to bruise. His face gave off no emotion. But I could feel them. Worry turned in him.

"Human, my name is Nola. I have great plans for you." "Knoc has informed me. I have decided to come willingly."

Nola smirked at me, and slowly walked towards me. Knocton tucked me slightly behind him. His body raged with concern. And something else, I couldn't place.

"Knoc? A nickname. I see you have grown attached to my nephew. Well, whatever he told you isn't true."

At that, Knocton completely pushed me behind him, his whole body going on the defense.

"What do you mean Uncle? What is going on?"

Nola laughed loudly. The laugh cut into me, and my whole body froze. I gripped onto Knocton's long cloak. I peeked out from behind him.

Darkness spilled from Nola's eyes, and when they dipped to me, his hunger gripped me. My body shook with fear.

"You see Nephew, you may be king by birth right, but you are not fit for king. Our planet was never dying of resources, or of our people. We have plenty of people. But those people are loyal to you. So, I needed to fool you, and make you think that our kingdom was in doom. I tricked you. And it was far easier than I thought. You are a genius like my sister, but you are as absent minded with family as your father. Your nose in a book and playing with the children of the village left you vulnerable."

Knocton's body tensed, and I felt a tremor rip through his body. I wrapped my arms around his waist. He needed comfort just as much as I did.

He gripped my hands with his own. His covered both of mine and sent warmth through me.

"This can't be. I trusted you. You are my mother's brother. How could you do this? What do you have planned for Molly?"

"Your mother was a friend of the people. She was a great queen. But she did not have a stern hand, neither did your father. The war that took them away, and killed most of our warriors was not by surprise. I let them in, Knocton. I told them about the weak point in the protection."

I felt Knocton's knees give. I dropped to his side. His head bent down, one knee on the ground and the other risen. His body trembled now. I watched as a tear hit his beautiful blue skin. His golden blonde hair covered his face.

Nola walked over, towering above us. A grin plastered his face. He was happy. My stomach churned. I glared at him. I held onto Knocton's shoulders.

"What had to be done, was done, Nephew. As so is this."

He reached down, and gripped my arm, pulling me away. I tried to kick and bite him. But he was too strong. Knocton's head shot up.

His eyes shined like the sun. He rose to his feet. I could feel his soul ache for mine. I reached my arms too him.

Chapter Seventeen

Knocton

My rage soaked me from the inside out. I watched Molly reach for me. The betrayal of Uncle had hit me as if I'd been physically attacked.

My body felt like a burning sun. Molly's eyes were pouring tears, and I needed her away from him.

"Now my plan. This human will bear my children. And my children and I will become the rulers of this weak kingdom. And as you know, I have ways to make each pregnancy fast. But unfortunately for her, she won't be alive by the time the last child is born."

Uncle smiled and licked her face. Hot rage seared through me. I could feel Molly plead with me to save her.

I stepped forward, but Uncle waved his finger at me.

"Now, Now Nephew. You don't want me to snap her pretty neck do you. I can keep her body fresh, and still have my children."

"Please, not her." I begged.

"Human, you have really done a number on my nephew. Captain, take us from this planet and to home."

The ship took a sharp turn, and then jerked forward. I watched it as Molly took the opportunity to free herself from his grip and run towards me.

But just as our fingertips touched, Nola came behind her. With a flick of his hand, sent her into the wall next to the captain's seats.

"MOLLY!" I pierced into the ship's air.

Uncle gripped my throat and held me in the air.

"I will have her alive or dead. I will have this kingdom. I am next in line. Faking a deadly accident death will be easy."

I stared over at Molly. Her crumpled body lay on her side. Her breathing was faint. My body screamed at me to break his hold and run to her.

I flew my hands into Uncle's eyes, stabbing my fingers into them. Uncle screamed dropping me. Black blood poured from them.

"You really think that a little stab to my eyes will stop me?"

Uncle came racing at me. A fist smacked into my cheek, and another followed into my gut. I dodged the next attack to my head and sent a uppercut into his chin. This sent him flying back. I stood over him.

Movement drew my attention away. Molly sat upright. Her nose bled and she held her side. I ran to her, leaving my uncle on the ground.

I held her cheek in my hand, wiping the blood from her nose. I placed my hand on her left side. Her ribs were broken on that side, but she smiled at me.

"I'm sorry, Molly. I should have seen through his plan."

"Family isn't supposed to betray you, Knoc. No need to apologize."

I closed my eyes and took her hands into mine. I kissed her knuckles. But when I found her eyes, they moved behind me.

And in an instant, as if she hadn't been injured, she threw herself over me. A sharp blade flew through her shoulder, inches above her heart.

She fell beside me. My heart shattered, and I felt every part of my body free fall, as if the ship broke apart into space. I began to shake. Hatred filled my bones. Tears poured onto her face.

I gathered her into my arms. Her blood soaked through my hands.

"No…No…Molly. Now why did you do that?" A faint smile played on her lips.

"In..my world..a hero…a king needs something to make him believe. A sacrifice, to make him a hero."

I shook my head at her. I didn't want her to die. I would have become a better king with her by my side if that's what she had wished for.

"No. I did not need saving. I'm more than human. I would have survived."

Molly smiled. Her blood ran through my fingers.

"Your body may…have not needed…saving but this did."

She lifted her finger to my heart and tapped. I wrapped my arms around her. Her body began to feel cold. I tried to share my warmth with her. I cried into her neck.

Chapter Eighteen

Molly

I felt weak, and my body felt as if I were trapped in ice. Knocton's eyes were pouring with sorrow and tears. His warmth tried to embrace my body, but I couldn't feel much of it. My body felt numb.

The sword went into my shoulder, barely missing my heart. But still, there was so much blood.

"Nephew, you are showing weakness to an enemy. The girl has more strength than you. She took a blade for you. Get up and fight. Die alongside her and die like a king. Like your parents, by my hand." Nola smirked.

Knocton removed his face from my neck. His eyes looked down into mine with love. I realized then that I grew to love this being. I didn't understand the plan he had at first even if it was a lie now.

But he showed me kindness. He showed me regret from his actions. I grew up without people feeling regret for using or beating me, for abandoning me. But he did, and I felt all of it.

He laid my broken body on the ground beside him. He took the arm from his cloak and ripped it off. He tied it around my wound, leaving the blade.

The tightness of the cloth trapped the blood. I let out a whimper. The wrapping stung, but it helped the bleeding slow. but would it stop it?

"She is human, Knocton. Wrapping a wound like that won't save her."

Knocton kissed my cheek, and slowly stood. On the wall behind us was a row of swords. He grabbed one from it and positioned himself for a fight.

"It may not save her, but it will buy her time. I will kill you. I will take her to Akrane to heal. and I will bring her back to Oliver, to her family. Even if it's to say goodbye. And if so, be it, I will allow them to kill me. I'll allow my blood to be shed with hers." "So be it, Nephew." Nola laughed.

I watched as they fought. Nola seemed more trained with sword fighting and landed more blows. I worried about Knocton. I could imagine him avoiding combat training, preferring to stay inside the pages of a book.

Or maybe skipping classes on histories of their wars to star gaze. I could see Knocton for who he really was. He was a gentle being. One that would do anything to protect his people, but also think of those who he'd have to go through to get that help.

My mind raced while they fought. My body became completely numb now. I could still feel the seeping of my blood, but it no longer rushed from me.

I thought of Oliver, and how mad he would be at me or maybe at himself. But knowing him, he will blame himself. And if so, I hope Parker will be there to comfort him. Memories of my childhood flooded my mind.

Bad ones more than good. A small tear rolled down my cheek. I don't think I'll be remembered for much. I was just a small journalist. I wrote many articles, and I was good at my job, but I never did anything to be remembered by.

A loud thud broke through my thoughts. I turned my eyes. towards them. Knocton lay on the ground, the sword hovering over him. I gasped, wanting to crawl to him, to somehow help.

"What did I tell you when you skipped those combat lessons Nephew? You would need them one day. If only you knew it was for me. The truest enemy you'd ever face. Now I give you an option. Surrender the throne to me, live but be kept in our dungeons as you go insane, or die with the human?"

"To live in a dungeon for the rest of my long life is not living." Knocton spat.

"Hmmm…I see. Death it shall be."

I watched as he moved the sword above his head, to smash it into Knocton. The only thing I could manage to do was yell.

"FIGHT LIKE A KING, KNOC!"

Chapter Nineteen

Knocton

Molly's words rang into my ears. The thing I needed to hear most. I needed to fight like a king. I needed to protect my people from this monster. And I needed to keep my promise to Molly.

I dodged his blow and swiped my leg at him. He tripped and landed on his face. I jumped at him, crushing my boot on his hand. The sword slid and the crunch of his bones filled my ears. Uncle grunted under my boot.

"What now Nephew? Do you even have the strength to kill family?"

"You were once my family. Why did you do it? Why did you kill them? Our people, your sister?"

Uncle took a moment to respond, and when he did, the biggest and toothy grin spread across his bruised red skin.

"Your mother and father were weak beings. Your mother had always been. Yes, she was a warrior princess from the day she was born. But she was too soft. That's why she chose your father. He made her laugh and treated her as an equal. You know in our customs, you can either marry your brother or someone from another planet. We would have ruled much better. I would have been her king."

My eyes were wet once again. His words stung me to the core. Molly's coughing stopped my thoughts. I turned my eyes to her.

Her skin had paled even more, and her breathing was fainter. Her eyes half lids, staring at me. "Looks like your little human is barley holding on."

My nerve broke, and I flew the sword through Uncle's throat.

"HER NAME IS MOLLY!"

His blood sprayed my face and hands. I let the sword slip from my grasp. Uncle's face was in frozen shock, and his body twitched as he died. We may take longer to die, but we can be killed. I raced to Molly. Her skin was ice cold, and her eyes were weak.

"Hold on Molly. I can easily get Oliver here. It will be faster to see my healer."

There were still some of our extra captains on board. They were asleep in the bottom of the ship. I radioed them in, and seconds later they arrived. They stared in horror at Uncle's body and back at me.

"There is no time. I will explain once I finish my final mission."

They nodded and jumped into the seats.

"Turn on the teleport. Here."

I handed a hair to one of the captains. They placed it in the teleport machine. The tube lit up and in seconds a scared Oliver appeared. His face paled and his whole presence shook.

He took in the scene then landed his eyes on Molly and me. He banged on the tube. The captains let him out and he raced to us. He touched her gently.

"What the hell happened? Where are we? Wait, you are blue! Are you an alien? Are you the ones from the news report?"

"A true journalist." *Molly laughed quietly.*

"Molly, what happened?" Oliver asked.

"His uncle wanted to kill him and use me." Her voice was barely a whisper.

Molly was fading and I needed to get home. I could save her there. My technology outdid what the earth had.

"Her body is in shock. We need to stabilize her before the sword is withdrawn, my king."

I nodded at my captains. I felt sick to my stomach. Oliver paced beside me. He chewed on his fingernails, and tears ran down his face.

"Oliver, my doctors are much more advanced than earths. We will take her there."

---  ---

With our technology, Arkane arrived quickly. Molly still hung on, but her time was coming near. The captains landed the ship outside of Arkane.

I gently lifted Molly into my arms. She was so drained of energy; she made no cry of pain. Before we stepped out, I placed oxygen masks on Oliver and Molly.

I could feel her life force slowly pouring from her. My soul cried out to her, and my heart broke. I made my way down the stairs.

Our technologies don't end just on our ships. We are far more advanced than humans.

I clicked my watch, making sure not to move so much to hurt Molly further. This sent my signal out to the workers and doctors. Soon servants and our doctors came gushing out to me. They stilled when their eyes fell upon Oliver and Molly.

"Doctors, please take her and begin surgery. The rest, please retrieve my uncle from aboard. Burn his body."

"Yes, my king." They all replied.

I looked down at Molly. She stared back and nodded.

"Here you are, little morning star."

I whispered kissing her forehead.

I placed her on a gurney, and we raced with the doctors to the operation area of the castle.

---   ---

Oliver paced as they finished wrapping the wound.

"Is it true? What she just said." Oliver spoke as we paced.

I stared off at Molly. They had stabilized her, and now was wrapping her wound. I could see she was coming out of sleep.

"Yes unfortunately. My parents ruled before me. They had taught me gentleness, trust and kindness. They told me, family wouldn't hurt family. But they were wrong. That lesson failed."

Oliver studied me for a moment. His nerves seemed to have shimmered down.

"What is your plan now then?"

"If you mean Molly. I plan to return her."

"What? What about your land, your people?

"They were never in any danger. He lied. I took Molly out of a selfish cause. I was going to use her. Even my way would have been gentle, even out of love."

Oliver turned his attention to Molly. The nurses headed out of the room, while two doctors stayed.

"I know Molly. I've known her all my life. She wouldn't have let you use her. If she put her life before her own, you have a place in her heart."

"So that may be. But she is not mine to keep." I sadly smiled.

Chapter Twenty

Molly

I fluttered my eyes open. Oliver sat on the bed next to me, reading. My shoulder ached but I did it, I didn't die. Knocton saved me.

"Ollie?"

Oliver looked down at me. His eyes were bloodshot and tired.

He hugged me so tight, and my arm jerked.

"Easy."

He pulled away.

"I'm sorry Molly. I should have believed you. This place is out of the Xfiles."

I smiled at him. He looked so tired. Grey bags hung under his eyes. But those lovely blue eyes were still bright.

"It's okay. I'm okay. Where's Knoc?" Oliver's smile faulted for a moment.

"He had to address his people. But he should be done now. Want me to get him?"

I nodded. Oliver went to the door, asking the guard for Knocton. He closed the door and looked at me.

"I am not gonna lie. But this whole thing has been mind shattering."

"It seems you're holding it together well."

His eyes stared into the floor. He seemed heavier. My Oliver always had a light presence.

"I'm not sure. It's a lot to take in. I almost lost you."

 "But you didn't."

He nodded. He rushed over, grabbing my hands.

"Did you fall in love with an alien?"

His words struck me.

I didn't know how to reply but he didn't give me the chance.

"My Molly wouldn't agree to be used. She would let herself die, especially for someone she loved." "Hey, I would save a stranger too you know. Remember that kid I saved from being hit by a bus?" Oliver smiled at me. "You know what I mean. You love him."

"I barley know him."

"Sometimes the fairy tales are true. The tug in our very souls when we collide with that person or feel the emptiness when they leave. It's love. No matter if we've known them for a day or a lifetime."

"So, the photographer becomes a writer." I nudged him.

The door opened and a guard walked in.

"I have the king."

"Come in."

The guard opened the door, and Knocton walked in. He wore different robes this time. White silk shaped his body. His hair was pulled in a messy bun.

"How are you, Molly?"

"My shoulder aches. But thanks to you, I'm alive."

He smiled, and my heartbeat faster.

"Does this place have normal food?"

"Oh yes. The guard can show you."

Oliver leaves us, and Knocton sits gently beside me.

"How are you, Knoc?"

"I'm not sure. My kingdom is a bit shaken."

"Are they wanting a new king?" Knocton giggled.

"No, never. My people love me. We are family. We just must heal."

I grabbed his hands and stared into his eyes. Maybe I did love him in a short time.

"Molly, I must put my kingdom before me."

He squeezed my hands. I pulled myself up, sitting towards him, wincing. I cupped his face.

"Knoc, you are king. A beloved king. I am just a human being. You live longer than me. Do what you must. It will be okay." I hugged him tightly.

"I'll miss you dearly."

"Fate is a fickle thing. But it knows what we need more then ourselves."

A knock echoed through the room, breaking our hug. The guard ushered Oliver in. Knocton kissed my cheek and stood.

"Let's get you two home."

Chapter Twenty-One

Knocton

I watched as we flew through space. My heart ached. I wanted to ask her if she would stay with me. To teach of her kind, to show me their way of life. Give me her lifetime with so I can love her even longer.

But she was a wild bird, and I couldn't keep her caged. My thoughts were interrupted by small footfalls. I turned around to see Molly slowly walking towards me.

Her arm was in a sling, and she looked worn. I ran over to her, taking her arm in mine and leading her to my throne.

"Oh, what an honor to be allowed seated on a king's throne." *She giggled.*

I smiled at her, and my heart skipped a beat. I would miss this human dearly.

"Also sometimes fit for a queen."

"Well yes. A queen."

She looked out the windows and stared.

"You know, I never believed in God, angels, the devil or much outside of the realm that was invisible. But now, I knew I was wrong. You are real, maybe the rest of it is too."

"Maybe it is. There is more than the reason of comfort that every species has a god, or gods in their cultures."

I watched as her mind pondered on my words. Her eyes shined on my favorite shade of emerald, and another crack broke through my heart.

"You have a point, my king." *She smiled.*

I nodded and stared out the windows as well.

"How much longer?"

"That eager to get back to your mundane human life?" I laughed.

She smiled, but it didn't reach her eyes. There was a touch of sorrow behind them.

"About thirty minutes. You should go rest Molly. You'll have a lot of explaining to John for Oliver. It seems only hours here. But it's days on Earth."

She rose from the throne and stood in front me.

She suddenly drew me in for a kiss. I wrapped my arms tightly around her, careful not to press against her arm.

Our lips synced perfectly, she fit into like a glove. I never wanted to let her go, but I knew I had too. I watched a guard lead her back to my room.

Chapter Twenty-Two

Molly

"Are you alright?" Oliver asked.

"You know, I should be. I was kidnapped and almost used as a baby machine by a madman. But also, by this beautiful kind creature. Now, I'm not. I should feel relief. We are going home. Life will be normal. But I can't seem to shake this ache inside my chest." Oliver smiled and held my left hand.

"Of course, it would be a magical man to capture the heart of my wildfire sister. A normal man would never have been a match for you."

Tears seeped from my eyes.

"What a shame right?"

Oliver nodded and took me into a soft hug.

A knock came to the door and a guard opened it.

"We are landing on the outskirts."

We nodded and watched as he closed the door. My heart shook in pain. I didn't want to go, but I couldn't leave the ones I also loved here. It wouldn't be like moving a state away, not even a country.

"Come on Molly. I'll be here."

I smiled and grabbed his hand. We walked to the control room of the ship, and Knocton stood waiting. I looked up at him. His sorrow was just as seen as mine was.

He walked us down the stairs, and we stood in the field. Oliver walked away from us, giving us a moment.

"It has been a time, Molly."

"You have no idea."

"I am so sorry for all of it."

I laughed, a real one. He didn't realize how much I grew to love him, or how much my heart needed him.

"This has been the best adventure I could ever have. I will never forget it. But will I ever see you again? Will we ever speak again?"

I stared at him, watching for any hidden answer behind those beautiful amber eyes.

Chapter Twenty-Three

Knocton

She asked me a question I knew I couldn't answer honestly. I watched as hope spun in her eyes. I wanted to say yes, but for now I knew I wouldn't be able to see her for a very long time.

"Molly, there may be worlds between us but one day we may meet again."

"Alright then I will hold you to that. We have an action that secures a promise you can't break. Here."

I watched as she held out her pinkie finger. She grabbed mine and wrapped it around hers. I chuckled.

"What a silly truce."

"So now, you must come back to see me. No matter where or how I am. Do you understand?"

"I understand. But I may not be back for a very long time. My kingdom needs their king through this time of mourning. I need to be a stronger king."

"I know. But come back to me someday, Knoc."

I smiled at her. I bent down and placed a kiss on her cheek.

"I will see you again, I promise."

She nodded, and I started up the ship's stairs. Oliver came running back to her side. Tears ran down her face, and my heart shattered. The doors closed, and as my ship rose in the air, she waved goodbye.

And without her saying anything, I heard "I love you."

50 Years Later

Molly (81 years of age)

I am an old woman now. Oliver passed away quite a while ago. Parker and I stood at his last intake of breath.

He lived a happy life and married the man of his dreams. I'm still waiting for my being from another time and world. It's been fifty years since we said goodbye. I hope he comes soon because I can feel my end nearing.

It's night, and I'm lying in my bed at the retirement home. The night has fallen, and I can feel it coming. They say death is a scary end.

But with the life I lived, it's a nice closing on a chapter of a wonderful life. I never married or had children. But I watched and helped Oliver's children grow.

We had a wonderful time at LCP. John passed a few years after Knocton dropped us back. I became the head of LCP.

I retired some time ago and passed it onto Oliver's oldest daughter, Lynn. My life has been good. My eyes feel heavy, and I'm about to fall asleep, when I feel a presence appear like magic in my old room. I know exactly who it is. My heart would know only him. I forced my eyes to see clearer. He pulls a chair next to my bed.

He has changed a bit. His azure skin is still bright, his stars still shine. And those amber eyes still illuminated the night. I smiled at him, and he smiled back.

"I thought you forgot."

"I would never break a truce. I am a king remember?"

I laughed, but a cough jerked me violently. He held my hand and sadly looked over me.

"Nola was right about one thing. Us humans are weak fragile creatures." I smiled weakly.

"Bodies mean nothing. Your heart will always be the strongest."

My body felt heavy, my time was drawing near.

"I can feel it, Molly. I wish I could come sooner. Spent more time with you." I grabbed his hand.

"Your people and kingdom come first. You came and kept your promise. That is all that matters. But I'm afraid, we don't have much time." He nodded.

"Then let's make this ending the best one, shall we?" I smiled with all I could. I watched as he pulled a small device out. It looked like a weird watch. He strapped it onto my wrist. My body felt weird, and suddenly I was floating. I looked at him in surprise.

"This will float you, but not keep you alive. I want one last moment with you, how we used to."

He took my hand and materialized us out of the home. We floated up into the skin. He held me there.

"I am so old compared to you. The beautiful girl you left has been gone for years."

I rested my head on his chest.

"No. I still see her. Growing old is a beautiful thing. All the things you have seen, and all the adventures, all the family. You lived a life of love. Nothing could be more beautiful than that. And these last moments will be the ending to a beautiful story."

We floated there for a few minutes when I felt my life force slowly draining. Only a few minutes now.

"I have loved you my whole life, Knocton." He tilted my head up.

"I will love you my whole lifetime, my sweet morning star."

And with that, it seemed it was my release. I laid my head on his chest, and everything went black. This life was gone. I felt my soul leave and float into the stars, into Knocton.

Afterword

Thank you for taking your time reading this short story!
I put a lot of time and love into this story, and the characters.
Please look out for future stories on Kindle, and Barnes and
Noble Press.
With All My Love,
Marley O'Connor